For Matt and Leo,

with my love.

A new day begins.

CANDLEWICK PRESS

First U.S. edition 2019
First published by Walker Books Ltd. (U.K.) 2019

Library of Congress Catalog Card Number 2018962288
ISBN 978-0-7636-9606-1

19 20 21 22 23 24 CCP 10 9 8 7 6 5 4 3 2 1

Printed in Shenzhen, Guangdong, China

This book was typeset in Poliphilus MT.
The illustrations were done in graphite and charcoal and colored digitally.

Candlewick Press
99 Dover Street
Somerville, Massachusetts 02144

visit us at www.candlewick.com

Right at the top
of Shiverhawk Hall
live children in pictures
on the wall.

Peeking out, woken gently
by a midsummer moon,
they spot something strange
about their room:

the twins have vanished
from their picture frame!
Where could they be?
It's time for a game. . . .

"HIDE AND SEEK!" cries Percy.

Lily says, "Whoopeee!"

"Let's find the twins!"
say the Plumseys, all three.

Billy starts the countdown
while the others look for clues.
"10-9-8-7-6-5-4-3-2-1 . . .

"WE'RE COMING

TO FIND YOU!"

The friends run wild through the warm night air,

hunting for white ribbons and long black hair.

"I've found the twins! Look up here!" says Lily,
and Percy says, "Those are just statues, silly!"

Then the splashing begins and no one can see

two clever girls hiding, quiet as can be.

Squeezing out through the wall, they find their way
and there, in the wild of the woods, they play.

Spying birds up above, spotting bugs down below,

but no sign of the twins, so onward they go . . .

until they arrive at the best place of all! "Let's play here forever!" the children call.

Then all of a sudden there's a sneeze from the bushes! Some giggling, too!

What could it be? Could it be you-know-who?

Percy gasps, hops closer, and—

"FOUND

The Shiverhawk children
have found their two friends.
"My turn now!" cheers Percy.
"Let's play it again!"

But just at that moment
the sky starts to tremble,
to rumble,
to CRASH!

And—
plip
plop
    plip plop
plip *plop* *plip* *plop* *plip* *plop* *plip* *plop* . . .

A thunder bolt, a lightning flash!
"Oh, no! We're so far from home!
It's time to get back!"

So they slip and squelch back through their forest of fun,

waving *Bye-bye, birds! Bye-bye, bugs!* as they run.

With muddy wet ribbons and soggy black hair,

the two lead their friends through the damp dawn air.

The twins are first in,
scrambling up to their room,
then it's Lily, then Billy,
then the Plumseys, and soon

they call down to Percy,
"Be quick! Climb in!"

And the rain starts to soften—
plip plop
  plip
    plop
      plip.
The sun's on its way;
a new day will begin.

And so into their frames
the children sneak,
till the next time they play . . .

hide and seek.